To order additional copies of this book, contact:
Xlibris
844-714-8691
www.Xlibris.com
Orders@Xlibris.com

ISBN: 978-1-6698-1882-3 (sc)
ISBN: 978-1-6698-1883-0 (e)

Print information available on the last page

Rev. date: 03/31/2022

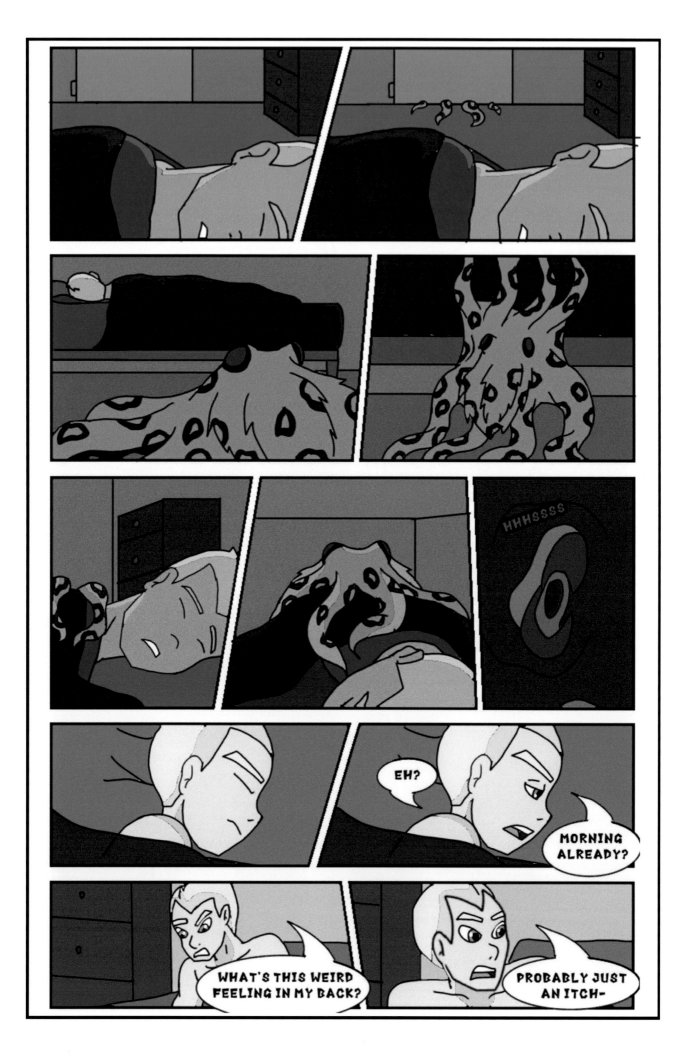

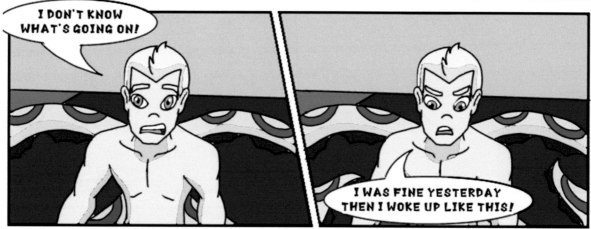

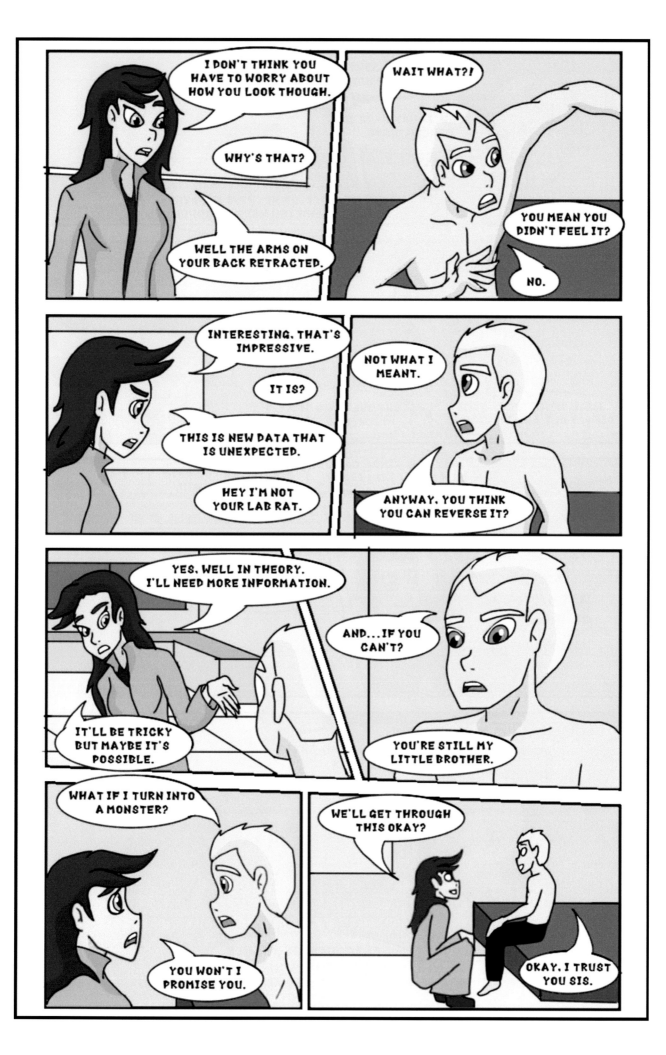

Issue #2

BLUE - RINGED OCTOPUS

NEXT ISSUE : " PISTOL SHRIMP "

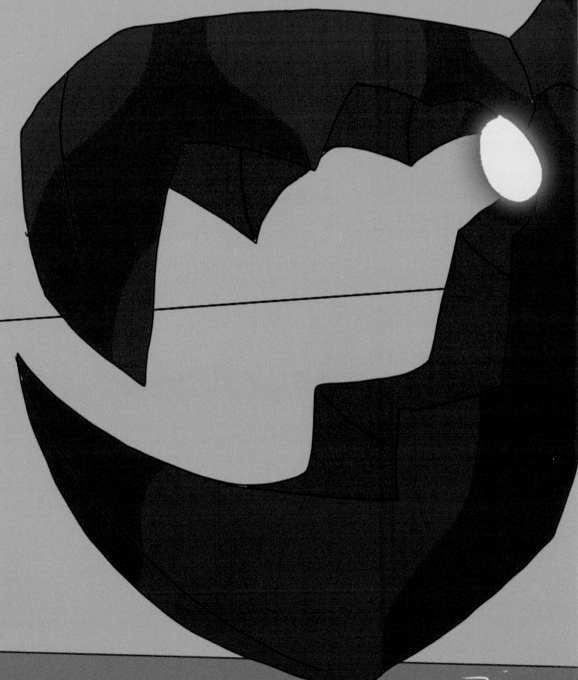

**CREATED BY
DEION TILLETT**

Printed in the United States
by Baker & Taylor Publisher Services